...THERE **MUST** BE SOME **MISTAKE!** I'M PROGRAMMED FOR **ETIQUETTE,** **NOT** **DESTRUCTION!**"

STAR WARS

THE SECRET LIFE OF
DROIDS

WRITTEN BY
JASON FRY

CONTENTS

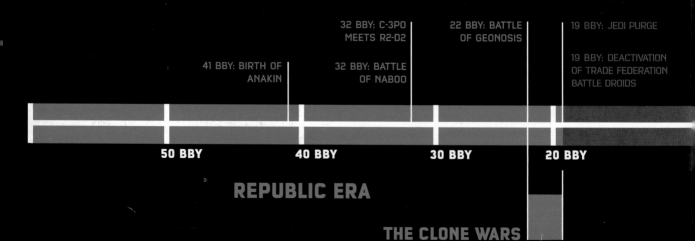

■ Droids are full of surprises. Throughout the book, look out for extra details about droids in special boxes like this.

Most droids don't take sides: they simply obey their master. But some droids are built to wage war, and their brains are programmed to be loyal to their cause. During the Clone Wars, the Separatists deploy an enormous Droid Army, made up of thousands of battle droids who will stop at nothing to defeat their enemies.

32 BBY: C-3PO
MEETS R2-D2

22 BBY: BATTLE
OF GEONOSIS

19 BBY: JEDI PURGE

41 BBY: BIRTH OF
ANAKIN

32 BBY: BATTLE
OF NABOO

19 BBY: DEACTIVATION
OF TRADE FEDERATION
BATTLE DROIDS

50 BBY   **40 BBY**   **30 BBY**   **20 BBY**

REPUBLIC ERA

THE CLONE WARS

DROIDS

Droids are everywhere! They can be found in all corners of the galaxy, working hard at their tasks. There is a droid for every job—whether it's delivering messages, spying, cooking, piloting starships, or fighting wars.

Most droids can do only what they are programmed to, although sometimes faulty wiring can cause trouble. Droids usually go about their tasks without complaining, but some droids are fussier than others.

Droids can surprise you. Can they keep secrets? Trick their enemies? Do they ever make friends? Fire up your data receivers and discover the secret life of droids!

NOTE ON DATES: Dates are fixed around the Battle of Yavin in year 0. All events prior to this are measured in terms of years Before the Battle of Yavin (BBY). Events after it are measured in terms of years After the Battle of Yavin (ABY).

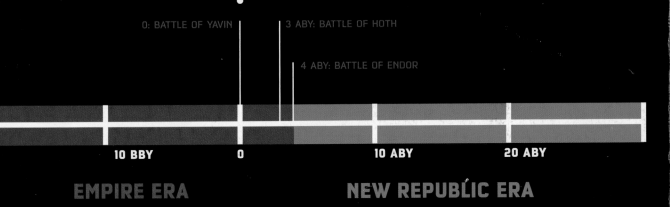

0: BATTLE OF YAVIN

3 ABY: BATTLE OF HOTH

4 ABY: BATTLE OF ENDOR

10 BBY   0   10 ABY   20 ABY

EMPIRE ERA   **NEW REPUBLIC ERA**

DROIDS

The galaxy is home to droids of all shapes and sizes. Some are friendly and high-functioning, while others are dull and simple. Droids live and work together with millions of living beings—but what makes them different from life-forms?

- **BUILT**

- **PROGRAMMED WITH SKILLS**

- **REPAIRED EASILY**

- **CAN'T SENSE THE FORCE**

MADE TO SERVE

Droids are built in factories and programmed to serve a particular function. Few ever learn to think of themselves as individuals because they often have their experiences erased by a memory wipe.

LIFE-FORMS

BORN ■

MUST LEARN SKILLS ■

HEAL SLOWLY ■

CAN SENSE ■
THE FORCE

BORN TO DREAM
Most life-forms are born knowing very little, and spend years learning and forming memories. Most think about the future, and make choices to decide what they will accomplish during their lives.

WHAT ABOUT CLONES?
The Republic's clone troopers are living beings, but they share some similarities with droids. They are created in vats, age more quickly than ordinary humans, and their brains have been manipulated to make them good soldiers. Some life-forms think of clones as living droids.

11

Types of DROID

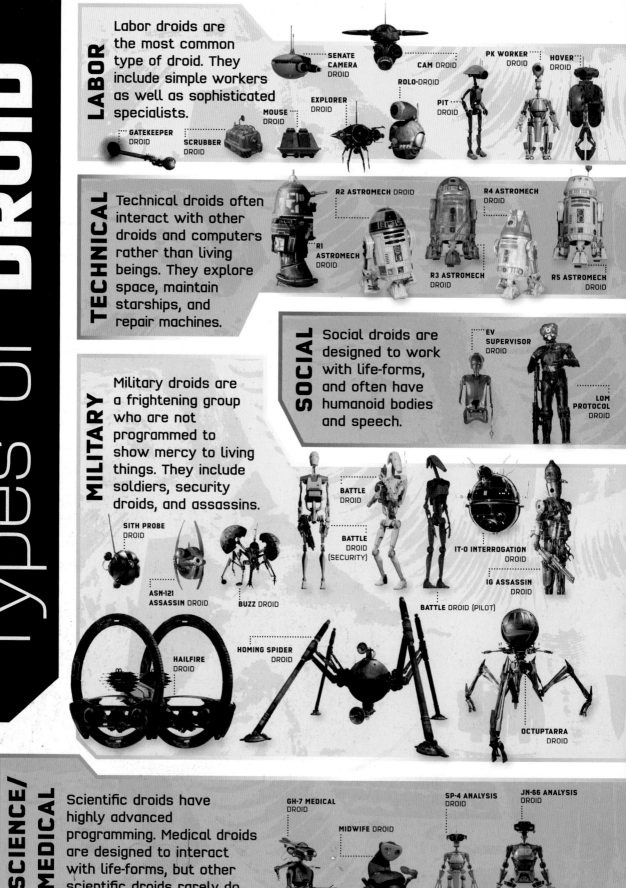

LABOR

Labor droids are the most common type of droid. They include simple workers as well as sophisticated specialists.

- GATEKEEPER DROID
- SCRUBBER DROID
- MOUSE DROID
- EXPLORER DROID
- SENATE CAMERA DROID
- CAM DROID
- ROLO-DROID
- PIT DROID
- PK WORKER DROID
- HOVER DROID

TECHNICAL

Technical droids often interact with other droids and computers rather than living beings. They explore space, maintain starships, and repair machines.

- R1 ASTROMECH DROID
- R2 ASTROMECH DROID
- R3 ASTROMECH DROID
- R4 ASTROMECH DROID
- R5 ASTROMECH DROID

SOCIAL

Social droids are designed to work with life-forms, and often have humanoid bodies and speech.

- EV SUPERVISOR DROID
- LOM PROTOCOL DROID

MILITARY

Military droids are a frightening group who are not programmed to show mercy to living things. They include soldiers, security droids, and assassins.

- SITH PROBE DROID
- ASN-121 ASSASSIN DROID
- BUZZ DROID
- BATTLE DROID
- BATTLE DROID (SECURITY)
- IT-0 INTERROGATION DROID
- IG ASSASSIN DROID
- BATTLE DROID (PILOT)
- HAILFIRE DROID
- HOMING SPIDER DROID
- OCTUPTARRA DROID

SCIENCE/MEDICAL

Scientific droids have highly advanced programming. Medical droids are designed to interact with life-forms, but other scientific droids rarely do.

- GH-7 MEDICAL DROID
- MIDWIFE DROID
- SP-4 ANALYSIS DROID
- JN-66 ANALYSIS DROID

PANNING DROID

BINARY LOADLIFTER

GNK POWER DROID

ORE EXTRACTION DROID

ELECTROREFINING DROID

MAINTENANCE DROID

FA-4 PILOT DROID

RIC RICKSHAW DROID

MINING DROID

PINCER DROID

VIPER PROBE DROID

TREADWELL DROID

WED DROID

SRT DROID

TC PROTOCOL DROID

TC PROTOCOL DROID

TC PROTOCOL DROID

CZ SECRETARY DROID

RA-7 PROTOCOL DROID

3PO PROTOCOL DROID

WA-7 WAITRESS DROID

BD-3000 LUXURY ASSISTANT DROID

DROIDEKA

SUPER BATTLE DROID

DWARF SPIDER DROID

CRAB DROID

IG-100 MAGNAGUARD

VULTURE DROID

DROID TRI-FIGHTER

TANK DROID

FX MEDICAL DROID

FX MEDICAL DROID

"CHOPPER" DROID

2-1B SURGICAL DROID

Astromech DROIDS

PRIMARY PHOTORECEPTOR
AND RADAR EYE

Astro-droids are a starship pilot's best friend. These useful little droids keep an electronic eye on flight performance, make repairs, target enemies during space battles, and do the complex math required to plan jumps through hyperspace.

R4-P44

JEDI HELPER
A cautious droid, R4-P17 serves as Obi-Wan Kenobi's astromech until buzz droids destroy her during the Battle of Coruscant.

PROCESSOR
STATE INDICATOR

ACOUSTIC
SIGNALLER

R4-P17

REPUBLIC DROID
R4-P44 assists Obi-Wan Kenobi's clone troopers during the Clone Wars. He flies many missions in ARC-170 starfighters, helping the Republic's brave pilots battle the Separatists.

LOOKING GOOD

After R4-P17's destruction, R4-G9 becomes Obi-Wan's astromech. Other astromechs whistle jealously when they see her fancy bronze dome.

DANGEROUS DUTY

Before the Clone Wars, R2-D2 serves aboard Queen Amidala's Royal Starship along with many other astro-droids. When the ship is damaged while fleeing Naboo, R2 and his fellow astro-droids, R2-N3 and G8-R3, race to repair it!

R5-D4

MAJOR MALFUNCTION

R5-D4 is an older astromech model whose circuits often malfunction. He is sold by Jawa droid traders to Luke Skywalker's Uncle Owen. But with a pop and a burst of smoke, R5's motivator breaks, so Owen takes R2-D2 instead.

ASTROMECH DROID

MANUFACTURER: INDUSTRIAL AUTOMATON

HEIGHT: VARIES

GENDER: VARIES

FEATURES: HOLOPROJECTOR, COMPUTER INTERFACE ARM, FIRE EXTINGUISHER, LIFE-FORM SCANNER, REPAIRS DATABASE

WHAT HAPPENS WHEN YOUR STARSHIP IS DAMAGED?

AFTER THE TRADE FEDERATION invades Naboo, Queen Amidala tries to flee in her starship. Trade Federation battleships open fire, and one shot knocks out the ship's shield generator, leaving the ship vulnerable to enemy fire. A few more hits will destroy the starship! Astromech droids rush out onto the ship's gleaming hull to perform emergency repairs in space. They better hurry!

BUZZ DROID DEFEAT

Over the planet Coruscant, buzz droids swarm Obi-Wan and Anakin's starfighters, wreaking havoc with saws and grippers. The droids destroy Obi-Wan's astromech and damage his ship, but Anakin and R2-D2 fight off the buzz droids, enabling the Jedi to continue their mission.

DROID DATA

■ Astromechs' barrel-shaped bodies contain a variety of arms tipped with tools. These tools let them do everything from repairing starships to talking with computers.

SPACE RESCUE

R2-D2 and his fellow droids, R2-B1 and G8-R3, race to repair Amidala's ship as laser blasts burst around them. Only R2 survives, and with seconds left, he repairs the shield and saves the Queen!

STARSHIP DOCTOR

An astro-droid's primary function is to keep starships running properly, so that the pilot can concentrate on flying and fighting. R2 assists Anakin Skywalker on his starfighter and then, many years later, helps his son, Luke.

DANGER ON DAGOBAH

R2's circuits are shielded against water damage, so when he falls into the swamps of Dagobah, he is happy to swim along. That is, until he is swallowed and spat out by a hungry dragonsnake!

R2-D2

R2-D2 looks like any other astromech, but he sure doesn't behave like one! Decades without memory wipes have allowed him to develop a unique personality. He might speak in beeps and whistles, but his friends usually have no problem understanding him!

DROID STATS

MANUFACTURER: INDUSTRIAL AUTOMATON

HEIGHT: 0.96 M (3 FT 2 IN)

GENDER: MALE PROGRAMMING

ALLEGIANCE: REPUBLIC/REBEL ALLIANCE

FEATURES: TOOLS, SENSORS, STARSHIP PILOTING AND MAINTENANCE PROGRAMMING, REPAIRS DATABASE

AERIAL ADVENTURES
R2-D2's thrusters allow him to go places his treads can't take him. But they burn lots of fuel and often break down. By the time he meets Luke, his jets have been removed.

RADAR EYE AND PHOTORECEPTOR

ONBOARD LOGIC FUNCTION DISPLAYS

THRUSTERS MADE BY BROOKS PROPULSION DEVICES

ALL-TERRAIN TREADS

POWERBUS CABLES

FAITHFUL FRIEND
When Luke goes missing on Hoth, R2 knows it's too dangerous to venture out across the snowy planet in search of his master. He can only stand watch at the gate, using his sensors to hunt for the faintest sign that Luke is still alive.

CAN A DROID BE TRUSTED TO COMPLETE A MISSION?

DROIDS FOLLOW THEIR masters' orders, but there's a big difference between obeying simple commands and carrying out a secret mission. When Darth Vader's Star Destroyer captures Princess Leia's ship, she orders a little astromech to find Obi-Wan Kenobi. R2-D2 is a loyal droid and does everything he can to complete his mission.

DROID DATA

■ Some masters use a restraining bolt to prevent their droid from leaving a specific area. This allows the master to control it remotely or even shut it down.

SECRET MISSION

Princess Leia loads the Death Star plans into R2's memory and records a message for Obi-Wan Kenobi. R2's mission: find the exiled Jedi and make sure he hears Leia's plea for help.

LUCKY ESCAPE

R2-D2 and C-3PO flee in an escape pod. Imperial officers detect no life-forms aboard, assume the pod short-circuited, and hold their fire.

DETERMINED

To carry out his mission, R2-D2 tricks Luke into removing his restraining bolt. He then crosses Tatooine's dangerous deserts alone at night in search of Obi-Wan, before finally delivering Leia's message.

DIPLOMATIC DUTY

TC-4 serves Yeb Yeb Adem'thorn, a Senator of the Swokes Swokes species. TC-4 is programmed with extensive knowledge of the money-worshipping Swokes Swokes culture.

TC-4

DANGEROUS TASK

Nute Gunray is too cowardly to meet with the Jedi Qui-Gon Jinn and Obi-Wan Kenobi when they arrive to discuss the illegal blockade of Naboo. He sends poor TC-14 instead, who has no idea her masters plan to destroy the Jedi with poison gas and battle droids.

Protocol DROIDS

Protocol droids are programmed to assist Senators, ambassadors, and business executives. They translate unfamiliar languages and help their masters offer proper greetings during negotiations with beings from the galaxy's millions of different species.

C-3PO

ICY CONDITIONS

K-3PO is the coordinator of all droids in the Rebel Alliance, stationed at Hoth's Echo Base. C-3PO isn't fond of the white droid and complains that he has little personality.

K-3PO

FLEXIBLE MID-BODY SECTION

PROTOCOL DROID

MANUFACTURER: CYBOT GALACTICA AND OTHERS

HEIGHT: VARIES

GENDER: VARIES

FEATURES: HUMANOID APPEARANCE, COMPLEX LANGUAGES DATABASE, UNIQUE PERSONALITY MATRIX, POLITE DEMEANOR

SPY DROID

The Galactic Empire uses RA-7 protocol droids to spy on its own officers. While helping their masters, RA-7s secretly record what they are doing and report suspicious activity.

RA-7

BUILT TO TALK

C-3PO has had many adventures—and hasn't enjoyed any of them. He was programmed to help diplomats and translate alien languages, a job for a civilized droid. So why does he have to travel on those dreadful starships and have people shoot at him?

C-3PO

TOUCH SENSORS

AUDITORY SENSOR

MAIN RECHARGE SOCKET

SHINY BRONZIUM PLATING

Protocol droid C-3PO is fluent in more than six million forms of communication, and programmed to be polite and helpful. He travels with Padmé Amidala on diplomatic missions for the Republic Senate, and later helps Princess Leia as she seeks support for the Rebellion.

THANK THE MAKER
C-3PO doesn't remember this, but he was built by young Anakin Skywalker, using parts from several protocol droids.

GOLDEN GOD
The Ewoks think C-3PO is a god, thanks to his shiny, golden casings. He uses his ability to speak the language of the Ewoks to convince the tribe to join the Rebellion.

C-3PO
MANUFACTURER: CUSTOM-BUILT

HEIGHT: 1.73 M (5 FT 8 IN)

GENDER: MALE PROGRAMMING

ALLEGIANCE: REPUBLIC/REBEL ALLIANCE

FEATURES: DIPLOMATIC PROGRAMMING, KNOWLEDGE OF CULTURES AND LANGUAGES

WE'RE DOOMED!
C-3PO expects the worst in any situation, but he becomes annoyed when his friends say he worries too much. Why can't everybody understand how dangerous the galaxy is?

C-3PO hasn't always looked the same. Over the years, he's been on many adventures and served lots of different masters. His outer casings have changed several times, and tell a fascinating story.

BITS AND PIECES

While a slave on Tatooine, Anakin Skywalker secretly builds C-3PO from scavenged parts. Some of his parts were made more than 80 years earlier on the planet Affa, which has many droid factories.

REBUILT AA-1 VERBOBRAIN

POWERBUS LINKAGE CABLES

MAIN POWER RECHARGE SOCKET

TATOOINE SERVANT

Anakin's mother, Shmi, covers C-3PO's exposed parts with dull gray plating while the droid serves the Lars family. After Shmi's death, Anakin reclaims his old droid.

STRUCTURAL LIMB STRUT

RUSTED SHINPLATE

SENATOR'S SERVANT

Anakin gives C-3PO to Padmé Amidala as a wedding present. As a Senator's translator, C-3PO has to fit in at important meetings and fancy diplomatic parties, so Padmé refits him with gleaming golden plating.

WEAR AND TEAR

After the fall of the Republic, C-3PO's memory is erased. He now works for the Rebel Alliance and has a number of replacement parts, which were added whenever part of his casings needed repair.

OLFACTORY SENSOR

INTERMOTOR ACTUATING COUPLER

HIGH-TORQUE KNEE JOINT

REPLACEMENT DROID PLATING

QUEEN AMIDALA
R2-D2 serves the Naboo Royal House. One day, he saves Queen Padmé Amidala's life and permanently joins her staff.

R2-D2

This small astromech serves two royal houses, a moisture farmer, a Hutt crimelord, and two Jedi. He learns some of the galaxy's biggest secrets over the years, but he keeps them to himself.

BAIL ORGANA
After Padmé's death and Anakin's fall to the dark side, R2-D2 and C-3PO spend years serving Alderaan's ruling Organa family.

ANAKIN SKYWALKER
Padmé gives R2-D2 to Anakin as a wedding gift, trusting the little droid to keep her husband safe in his Jedi starfighter.

ANAKIN SKYWALKER
When Anakin returns to Tatooine, he reclaims the droid he built as a young slave.

PADMÉ AMIDALA
Anakin gives C-3PO to Padmé as a wedding gift, hoping the droid can help with her duties as a Senator.

SHMI SKYWALKER
When Shmi marries Cliegg Lars, she takes C-3PO to serve on the Lars moisture farm.

ANAKIN SKYWALKER
Young slave Anakin secretly builds C-3PO to help his mother Shmi around their hovel.

TWO DROIDS: MANY OWNERS

R2-D2 and C-3PO first met long ago, when they had different masters and lived on different planets. During the Clone Wars, the two droids were brought together again, eventually becoming a pair always owned by the same master.

JAWAS
Escaping capture on the *Tantive IV*, the droids wander the wastes of Tatooine, where a band of Jawas grab them.

LUKE SKYWALKER
After Owen is killed by Imperial troops, his stepson, Luke, becomes the droids' master.

PRINCESS LEIA
The droids accompany Bail's stepdaughter Leia—secretly, Padmé's daughter—on missions aboard her starship, the *Tantive IV*.

OWEN LARS
Moisture farmer Owen Lars buys the droids from the Jawas, not recognizing C-3PO, his family's old droid, with his gold plating.

JABBA THE HUTT
As part of a plan to save Han Solo, Luke gives the droids to the gangster Jabba the Hutt, who puts them to work as servants.

C-3PO

Constructed from salvaged parts, C-3PO has been owned by lots of very important people. A memory wipe, ordered by Bail Organa, leaves C-3PO unaware that he has witnessed crucial events in galactic history.

LUKE SKYWALKER
Rescued from Jabba, the droids continue to serve Luke and his friends on many more adventures.

HOW DO R2-D2 AND C-3PO HELP EACH OTHER?

R2-D2 AND C-3PO ARE TWO very different droids: R2 was designed to help pilots and engineers with their starships, while C-3PO helps diplomats and politicians do their jobs. But the two friends often find themselves thrown together in tricky situations. Luckily, their unique skills complement each other and they work together to get each other out of trouble.

DROID DATA

■ R2-D2 can speak only in standard droid language Binary—also known as Droidspeak. Yet, thanks to his high-level programming, R2 can understand a variety of other languages.

PICKING UP THE PIECES

C-3PO isn't a combat droid, and is terrified to find his head has been separated from his body—and welded onto a battle droid! Fortunately, R2 is able to put C-3PO's metal body back together, ignoring C-3PO's anxious complaints as he works.

R2 TO THE RESCUE!

R2-D2's wide assortment of tools means he can fix just about anything. When C-3PO is blasted apart on Cloud City, R2 happily fixes his friend. He just takes a short break to repair the *Millennium Falcon*'s hyperdrive, helping everyone on board escape from Darth Vader.

TRUE FRIENDSHIP

Few living beings can understand R2-D2's language of beeps and whistles, but C-3PO finds his friend's electronic noises easy to interpret. C-3PO often translates what R2 has to say, although he politely leaves out any comments that might be a bit too rude.

WATCH OUT FOR THE PIT DROIDS!

Pit droids are a common sight in Podracing arenas. The little droids are strong and never question orders—but they can also be a bit foolish. They like to have fun while doing their jobs, but they are often reckless, which sometimes leads to unfortunate accidents.

AIR TROUBLES

The thrusters on Ebe E. Endocott's Podracer need to be unblocked. While two pit droids argue about who will get on whose shoulders to do it, one activates a third's air gun, blasting a fourth with a burst of compressed air.

SOMETHING BORROWED

Ebe's air gun is out of power, so his droids borrow one from Ody Mandrell's crew. Ody's droids weren't using it, were they?

FULL OF BAD IDEAS

Pit droids are tough enough to survive almost any accident, so they never worry about getting damaged. But mechanics sometimes wish they did worry! The simple-minded droids have been known to think up some very foolish ideas, like trying to peer inside an engine while it's still running!

DROID DATA

■ Pit droids' mechanical fingers aren't good enough for intricate repairs, and their brains can't cope with complex tasks. Mechanics use them mostly for simple jobs.

WATCH YOUR STEP!

The thrusters need new baffles. A pit droid grabs an armload and rushes off—but he doesn't see the deactivated pit droid lying in his path...

HARD AT WORK?

Pit droids are strong enough to carry an afterburner, no problem. However, they don't need it to fix Ebe's Podracer, they just want to stand on top of it so they can reach the thrusters!

JOINTS ARE
VULNERABLE
POINTS

ROGER ROGER
Battle droid commanders are marked by yellow spots on their heads and chests. They order regular droids into battle using military strategies downloaded into their brain databases.

LIMBS FOLD FOR
TRANSPORT

ON GUARD
Security droids have red markings, but are functionally the same as regular battle droids. They are often assigned to patrol duties aboard Separatist warships.

Battle
DROIDS

Battle droids aren't smart, but they don't need to be! They are simple war robots programmed to follow orders and overwhelm enemies by attacking in huge numbers. Go ahead and blast them, the Separatists will just build more!

SECURITY DROID

BATTLE DROID

MANUFACTURER: BAKTOID
HEIGHT: 1.91 M (6 FT 3 IN)
GENDER: MALE PROGRAMMING
FEATURES: E-5 BLASTER RIFLE, SOME UNITS HAVE TOUGHER ARMOR AND SPECIALIZED PROGRAMMING

SIGNAL ANTENNA

SIMPLE VOCODER

BATTLE DROID

BATTLE OF NABOO

Evil Darth Sidious manipulates the Trade Federation into invading Naboo. Thousands of battle droids quickly occupy the green planet's cities and capture the Royal Palace.

E-5 BLASTER

TRIGGER HAPPY

Known as "clankers," battle droids become confused when they find themselves in situations for which they haven't been programmed. But beware: they often solve problems by firing their blasters.

DANGEROUS GOODS

The Trade Federation's enormous Droid Control Ships direct the movements of battleships, which are filled with assault vehicles, droid starfighters, and battle droids.

DROID SIGNAL RECEIVER STATION

UNINVITED GUESTS

During the invasion of Naboo, landing craft descend to the planet's surface and unload battle tanks and MTTs (multi-troop transports).

FOLDED BATTLE DROIDS

DROID PAYLOAD

Lots of heavily armored MTT carriers rumble from the landing sites to the battlefield. Each MTT opens its hatches to reveal storage racks holding 112 battle droids.

REPULSOR COOLING FINS

Preparing for **BATTLE**

When the Trade Federation decides to invade Naboo, it uses its experience transporting goods in freighters to move battle droids quickly into position and prepare them for war.

READY TO RUMBLE

The racks unload battle droids, still folded to save space. A signal from the Droid Control Ship tells the droids to unfold and prepare for battle, a process that takes less than 15 seconds.

- HEAD LOCKS IN PLACE AND DROID SENDS READY SIGNAL TO DROID CONTROL SHIP

- DROID DRAWS BLASTER AND AWAITS ORDERS

- IN STANDING POSITION, DROID PERFORMS MORE SYSTEM CHECKS

- ARMS AND LEGS UNFURL AND DROID CHECKS GYROSCOPIC SYSTEMS

- DROID DEPLOYED ON BATTLEFIELD, STILL FOLDED IN TRANSPORT MODE

WHY IS IT POINTLESS TO PLEAD MERCY WITH A BATTLE DROID?

BATTLE DROIDS ARE dangerous. Not only are they designed to destroy, but they also cannot think for themselves or question orders. Fortunately for clever Jedi and well-trained clone troopers, the slow-witted and physically weak droids are fairly easy to obliterate.

ONE MIND
Battle droids are programmed to have no emotions, so appealing to their sense of compassion is futile. Also, as identical robots, they all think the same—so asking for a second opinion will get you nowhere!

DOES NOT COMPUTE

Logic and reason mean nothing to battle droids. They lack the brain capacity to process any information that falls outside their narrow programming, so there's no point trying to have a discussion with them. When Obi-Wan tells the droids that he needs the ship they are guarding, their reaction to the unfamiliar information is to attack.

RELENTLESS

Once battle droids receive their orders, they will not stop until their mission is complete—or if they are destroyed.

HOW CAN YOU DEFEAT
BATTLE DROIDS?

THE TRADE FEDERATION'S battle droids are not the greatest individual soldiers, but their strength lies in numbers. The Gungans of Naboo fight bravely and are able to destroy individual battle droids quite easily, but they are vastly outnumbered. To truly defeat the Droid Army, the signal that controls the droids must be shut down.

■ After the Battle of Naboo, the Separatists reprogram some battle droids so they can move and fight without orders from a central computer.

LIGHTSABER POWER

Jedi like Qui-Gon Jinn make short work of battle droids with their lightsabers. But even a Jedi can't win when faced with thousands of these metal troopers.

DESTROY CENTRAL COMMAND

Naboo pilots fly into space and launch an attack on the orbiting Droid Control Ship. When young Anakin Skywalker blows up the ship, the computer controlling the battle droids is destroyed, too. In a second, the Trade Federation's terrifying army has been turned into silent scrap metal!

ONE LITTLE SHOVE

Without the signal from the Droid Control Ship, the battle droids shut down. All it takes is one little shove, and they fall to the ground. The delighted Gungans cheer as they push them over!

Super
BATTLE DROIDS

B2 Battle Droids—known as super battle droids—are the deadly frontliners of the Separatists' Droid Army. They are big, tough, and dumb. Super battle droids often march ahead of other Separatist droids, smashing through enemy troops and anything else that gets in their way.

BIG MISTAKE!
Super battle droids think smaller droids are weak and useless. This turns out to be a big mistake when two of them underestimate R2-D2, who squirts them with oil and sets them on fire using his thrusters. That'll teach them a lesson!

RAPID-FIRE DUAL LASER CANNON

COGNITIVE MODULE

MUSCLE MACHINE

The Separatists designed B2s to make up for the weaknesses of regular battle droids. B2s have stronger armor, more powerful blasters, and do not rely on a droid control signal.

FLEXIBLE ARMORED MIDSECTION

SUPER BATTLE DROID

MANUFACTURER: BAKTOID

HEIGHT: 1.93 M (6 FT 4 IN)

GENDER: MALE PROGRAMMING

FEATURES: SENSORS, COMMUNICATIONS GEAR, BUILT-IN BLASTERS

How Are DROIDS MADE?

Giant factories on the planet Geonosis produce new armies of battle droids for the Trade Federation. In the heat and noise of the factory, droids and Geonosian drones supervise assembly lines that never stop creating machines.

1 RAW MATERIALS

The Geonosians mine rock from the ring that surrounds their planet. Huge machines crush the rock, superlasers melt it, impurities are burned off, and the molten ore is poured from huge vats into molds, cooling to form droid parts.

HIVE WORKERS
Geonosians are insect-like beings who live in hives. Most Geonosian factory workers are drones that never question orders and barely think for themselves.

DROID DATA
- Geonosis's droid factory is actually quite small compared to the giant plants on ancient droid-making planets such as Affa, Mechis, Telti, and Cyrillia.

2 SUPERVISION

Geonosian workers and specialized droids keep a careful eye on the factory's assembly lines, looking for problems that could stop production. A SRT droid, which is normally used for transporting materials, will spot an unfamiliar droid and remove him from the conveyor belt.

"Machines making machines. How perverse."

C-3PO

3 CONVEYORS

Droid parts are stamped and finished and then speed around the factory on conveyor belts. As the parts go by, machines fuse them together and add more sophisticated systems.

4 KEEP MOVING!

Restarting the Geonosis factory's conveyors takes a long time, so the production line stops only if a big problem occurs. Small difficulties such as an incorrect head aren't worth halting the machines!

5 QUALITY CONTROL

Normally, a factory supervisor checks all completed droids and rejects any mistakes. But Geonosis is under attack, so even though a mix-up leaves C-3PO and a battle droid with switched heads and bodies, the batch is sent straight into combat!

DROIDEKA

MANUFACTURER: COLICOIDS
HEIGHT: 1.83 M (6 FT)
GENDER: NONE
FEATURES: ENERGY SHIELDS, RADIATION SENSORS

TROUBLE ON WHEELS
Droidekas travel by rolling; curling their arms, heads, and legs into a wheel. They then move with frightening speed to attack their enemies.

GEONOSIS ARENA
At the Battle of Geonosis, droidekas prove to be formidable opponents for the Jedi. But even their tough shields are no match against huge Republic gunships.

DROIDEKAS

Officially known as destroyer droids, these three-legged droids are some of the strongest units in the Separatist army. Clone troopers fear their powerful, rapid-fire cannons and impenetrable energy shields, and even Jedi Knights treat droidekas with respect.

PRIMARY SENSOR ANTENNA

SHIELD PROJECTOR PLATE

RAPID-FIRE LASER CANNON

SPECIAL DELIVERY
The vicious insect species known as the Colicoids created the early droideka models. As payment, they asked for 50 space barges full of exotic meat. Deal!

REACTOR HOUSING

RACKS OF MISSILES

MAGPULSE
DRIVE UNIT

ARMOR
PROTECTS
REACTOR

ARMORED
LIMBS

LASER
DISH

HOMING SPIDER DROID

These walking tanks use powerful
homing lasers to burn out shields
and melt armor. Republic soldiers
aim for their legs, which are the
most vulnerable points.

HAILFIRE DROID

Racks of missiles make this droid
tank a deadly opponent in battle.
Hailfires have little ability to think
for themselves, rolling into a fight
with a preprogrammed list of targets.

LASER CANNON

DWARF SPIDER DROID

Built to fight underground, dwarf
spider droids can see in the dark
and operate underwater. While not
incredibly smart, they can think for
themselves and sometimes
refuse dangerous missions.

BATTLEFIELD DROIDS

REACTOR
CORE

NOSE
LASER
CANNON

BUZZ DROID

These tiny saboteurs
swarm Republic
starfighters and damage
them. Some pilots crash
or get shot down after
trying crazy maneuvers
to dislodge the droids.

ARMOR-
PIERCING
DRILL

ION ENGINE

WING STRUTS

DROID
BRAIN

TRI-FIGHTER

Introduced late in the Clone
Wars, these droid starfighters
are heavily armed, fast, and
highly maneuverable. They
fight with blaster cannons,
missiles, and projectiles that
contain buzz droids.

DISCORD MISSILE
CONTAINS BUZZ
DROIDS

VULTURE DROID

Vultures aren't nearly as
effective as tri-fighters during
space battles, but are cheaper
to build and easier to repair.
They can fight on the ground
by walking on their wings.

COGNITIVE MODULE

ROTATING CANNON ASSEMBLY

CAN HANG UPSIDE DOWN

SENSOR STALKS

DURANIUM CLAWS

SENSOR BULB

HEAT EXHAUSTS

OCTUPTARRA DROID

These droids resemble animals from the planet Skako. They can see and fire in all directions. Some units are built with spray guns that release poisons or germs into the air.

CRAB DROID

Crab droids use their powerful limbs to scuttle over rocks or through swamps. However, their heads are poorly armored, and clone troopers have learnt to jump on top of them and fire at this weak spot.

The Separatists are afraid of getting injured, so they stay as far from the battlefield as possible, relying on droids to do their fighting for them. Many Separatist war machines are giant robots designed to fight independently on land and in space.

SENSOR PROCESSORS

MISSILE RACKS

ROTATING CANNON

TANK DROID

These snail-like tanks often protect hailfire droids or homing spiders. Their powerful armor lets them smash through walls or barriers to attack enemies with their deadly laser cannons.

DROID GUNSHIP

Droid gunships don't fight in outer space, but they are devastating enemies for Republic pilots battling in the skies. They fight with five laser cannons and racks of powerful missiles.

HOMING LASER

FUEL TANKS

OUTRIGGER TREAD

DRIVE AXIS HUB

WHY IS THE SEPARATIST ARMY SO POWERFUL?

THE SEPARATISTS HAVE several advantages in their war against the Republic: Firstly, they can overwhelm planets with huge numbers of battle droids. Secondly, they have lots of money to run enormous factories, which build new types of droids for different situations. Finally, the Separatist leaders can rest assured their droid troops will carry out orders without asking questions.

OUT OF HARM'S WAY

Separatist commanders transmit orders from large Droid Control Ships. Even if the battle droids on the ground are attacked, the command center remains safe in outer space, ready to regroup or deploy more droid soldiers.

DIVERSE DROIDS

The Separatists use many different kinds of droids, with models designed for battle on land, in the air, or under the sea. Tank droids, crab droids, and spider droids can even fight both on land and under water!

1 LAUNCH MISSILES!

Vulture droids and droid tri-fighters are armed with discord missiles, which pack seven buzz droids into an armored shell. Discord missiles are extremely fast and maneuverable, able to keep up with even the best Jedi star pilots.

BUZZ DROID
DEPLOYMENT

The deadly Colicoid species got the idea for buzz droids after seeing teams of tiny repair droids scuttle across freighters' hulls fixing problems. Buzz droids are programmed to create problems instead. Launched from speedy missiles, they swarm Republic starships, using mechanical limbs ending in drills, cutting torches, and saws to rip through metal hulls and systems, turning ships into flying scrap.

2 RELEASE THE DROIDS!

When a discord missile is close enough to a Republic warship or squadron of starfighters, it explodes, releasing buzz droids curled up inside protective spheres of armor.

3 TARGET ACQUIRED!

The buzz droids have simple sensors and small rocket jets for maneuvering. Once in space, they lock on to the nearest signal in hopes of finding a Republic ship to tear apart.

4 TIME TO OPERATE!

After locating a target, a buzz droid extends its legs and pops out of its shell, latching onto a ship with its magnetic feet. It scuttles along the hull until it reaches a weak point. Then it extends its pincers and arms and goes to work.

5 MISSION ACCOMPLISHED!

Buzz droids' memory banks are loaded with information about enemy ships, telling them where to strike. The droids work in swarms, tearing apart the ship's systems until their target has been reduced to a useless hulk of scrap metal, doomed to float forever in the emptiness of space.

WHY ARE VULTURE DROIDS SO DANGEROUS?

VULTURE DROIDS ARE frightening foes, both in space and on the ground. In space, these speedy droid starfighters swarm Republic ships like clouds of biting insects, overwhelming their defenses. On land, they can also transform into walking mode, using the tips of their wings like feet. In this configuration they guard warships and can even defend Separatist ground units.

HIGH SPEED

Vulture droids rely on simple strategies for space combat. They aren't as smart as living pilots, but their mechanical reflexes are much faster, and droid brains help them work together to fight enemy ships.

READY FOR LAUNCH
While in walk mode, Vulture droids patrol the hulls of Separatist warships instead of waiting in hangars. If enemy starfighters get too close, the droids only need a few seconds to switch to flight mode and launch.

A Day in the Life of a
DROID TRADER

Droid traders are always on the lookout for a bargain —or a foolish customer! Watto prides himself on having a keen eye for machines, the right touch with tools, and a shop overflowing with parts.

1 CLEAN UP JUNKSHOP

Watto's shop looks crowded and chaotic, but the Toydarian trader knows exactly where everything is. He'd be very angry if his young slave, Anakin Skywalker, messed it up!

DROID DATA

■ Watto was a soldier on the planet Toydaria before moving to Tatooine. He lived with a group of Jawas, learning their droid trading ways, before he set up his own junkshop.

2 FIND DROIDS TO SELL

Broken, abandoned droids are often found in Tatooine's towns or sold in pieces at a market stall. One look is enough to tell a smart trader whether a droid can be repaired or if it is just junk.

"No money, no parts, no deal!"
Watto

3 REPAIR DROIDS

Watto repairs broken droids using spare parts from his junkyard. His welding droid fuses metal together to make droids whole again and ready for sale.

4 OIL BATH

Once repaired, droids are dunked in an oil bath to stop them from creaking and to make them look shiny. A couple of oily spots can also hide damage that costs too much for Watto to fix.

5 HAGGLE

There's no point fixing things unless it brings in a profit. Watto drives a hard bargain with customers, particularly if he knows no one else in town has what they want.

DREAMS AND SCHEMES

Watto makes a decent living repairing and selling droids and other junk in Mos Espa, but he dreams of making one big sale that will turn him into a VIT—a Very Important Toydarian.

DROIDS FOR SALE

For every job, there's a perfect droid. Do you need a factory supervisor? A camera to record your Podrace? A cargo loader for all your heavy lifting? Look no further—a trusty mechanical helper is all you need!

HOVER LOADER
If you need to transfer cargo between ships and freighters, this strong, simple-minded droid won't let you down.

PK WORKER DROID
This durable droid can be programmed to perform the same tasks over and over again—no matter how dull!

BINARY LOADLIFTER
Programmed for heavy lifting and not much thinking, the binary loadlifter will make light of all your heavy loads.

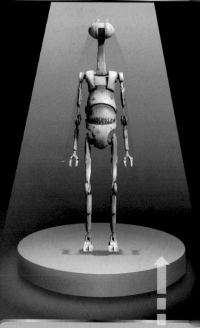

CAM DROID
Record important events with your very own camera droid! It can transmit crystal-clear footage to multiple viewscreens.

GNK POWER DROID
Never be without power again! This battery droid can supply energy to ships, machines, and other droids.

MAINTENANCE DROID
The Otoga-222 can perform a diverse variety of labor tasks. Designed to display curiosity, this droid is always learning.

PIT DROID
Fixing a Podracer is child's play for a pit droid! This strong droid is hard-working—and cheap!

SRT DROID
A welcome addition to any factory, the SRT droid moves bulk materials and supervises assembly lines.

ANALYSIS DROID
For all your data analysis needs, this droid boasts sensors and access to computer databases.

DEMOLITION DROID
Essential for any building site, this blast-proof droid sets and detonates explosives safely.

GATEKEEPER DROID
Keep unwanted visitors out with this popular droid. Equipped with a camera eye and voice box.

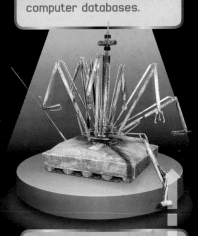

TREADWELL DROID
For the simplest repair jobs, look no further than the treadwell. Skilled and sturdy, it won't disappoint.

MOUSE DROID
This tiny droid will deliver your messages without fail. It can also stand guard or escort visitors.

ROLO-DROID
Need to keep an eye on your slaves? This modified PK droid will guard all your property with care.

EXPLORER DROID
Looking to explore alien worlds? This floating droid gathers and transmits a wide range of data.

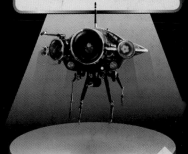

How to Choose
A DROID

Buying a used droid could save you money, but beware! Dishonest traders often sell damaged droids or machines with faulty programming. Make sure you choose your droid carefully.

1. SEE EVERYTHING FIRST

Before you start haggling, make sure you check out everything that's for sale, and never let a trader know what you're interested in. If you're too eager, a trader may hide a cheaper model at the back of the sandcrawler, so you are forced to pay more.

TREADWELL REPAIR DROID

2. ASK ABOUT ORIGINS

Ask where a droid came from, and see if you believe the trader's story. Or, if the droid can talk, ask it yourself. But remember, droids are sometimes programmed to lie. Is that protocol droid with the gold casing really an expert in programming binary loadlifters?

R2-D2

3. TAKE A CLOSE LOOK

A droid that looks fine on the outside can be a mess inside, so look out for frozen gears, loose wires, carbon-scoring, or a bad motivator. If a trader won't let you examine a droid closely, what is he trying to hide?

4. RETURN IF FAULTY

Ask for a guarantee that you can return the droid if something goes wrong. If there's a problem, don't delay—it's hard to get a refund or trade in a bad droid once the sandcrawler has rolled on to the next moisture farm.

"Uncle Owen! This Artoo unit has a bad motivator!"

Luke Skywalker

R5-D4

LIN DEMOLITIONMECH MINING DROID

WHY IS IT A
HARD LIFE
BEING A DROID?

VERY FEW OF the droids in the galaxy enjoy the freedom that most life-forms take for granted. Many droids are treated like slaves by their owners, then cast aside when they are no longer needed. The most a droid can hope for is that it will be bought by kind masters who will take good care of it.

ATTACKED IN BATTLE
War destroys millions of droids, whether they're combat droids built to fight in place of living beings, or astromechs caught in the middle of space battles. In the Battle of Coruscant, buzz droids tear off the head of poor R4-P17, Obi-Wan Kenobi's astromech.

OWNED BY OTHERS

Even kind masters can treat droids as property: C-3PO is shocked when Luke gives him and R2-D2 to Jabba the Hutt. He doesn't know that it's part of Luke's plan to rescue Han Solo.

CONSTANT DANGER

Some living beings like to torment defenseless droids, but sometimes droids are also cruel, or they do terrible things because of glitches in their programming. Beneath Jabba's palace is a grim dungeon where droids enjoy making other droids suffer. 8D8 is employed to terrify other droids. He uses heated metal to make a GNK power droid shriek with fear!

Service DROIDS

Service droids are designed to help living beings with small but necessary tasks. They must be able to communicate clearly and politely, and to follow instructions immediately.

FOR-HIRE HAULER

Despite their name, rickshaw droids are actually general-purpose labor droids used for many tasks, not just pulling carriages. Travelers should watch out for droids who are programmed to increase fares by taking roundabout routes.

RIC RICKSHAW DROID

POWERFUL GRIPPERS

SPACEPORT SERVANT

FA-5 droids are a common sight in spaceports, where they carry luggage and arrange transportation for travelers. They often bear the insignia of shuttle companies. Some FA-5s also work in private homes as butlers or servants.

WHISTLE FUNCTION FOR HAILING TRANSPORTATION

FA-5 VALET DROID

INDICATOR LIGHT SHOWS IF DROID IS FOR HIRE

BALANCE GYRO FOR DRIVE WHEEL

RAIN OR SHINE

Rickshaw droids often pull a covered carriage with seats for two. Travelers are relieved to find shelter from the sun or rain, while the droid rolls on, unaffected by the weather.

BD-3000 LUXURY ASSISTANT DROID

PLEASANT, CHARMING VOICE

MAGNETIC GRIPPER KEEPS TRAY IN PLACE

DECORATIVE SKIRT

WA-7 WAITRESS DROID

GLEAMING CHROMIUM FINISH

REPULSOR STABILIZER

CHROME CHARMER

BD-3000 droids typically work as secretaries, valets, nannies, or chauffeurs for politicians and busy executives. These gleaming robots are often programmed to flatter and charm visitors, but don't make assumptions: some BD-3000s have been reprogrammed as bodyguards or assassins.

DINER DYNAMO

WA-7 waitress droids rely on their gyro-balance circuitry to remain upright, even while carrying overloaded trays through crowds. Coruscant diner owner Dexter Jettster employed a talkative, sassy WA-7 unit nicknamed Flo.

DROID VISION: TECHNICAL

Not all droids see in the same way. What they see, and how well they see it, depends on what they are programmed to do. The visual capabilities of technical droids vary widely, from extremely basic, to multi-functional.

ENERGY DISTRIBUTION MODE

POWER LEVEL INDICATOR

POWER SOURCE DETECTION

DIRECTIONAL INDICATOR

OBSTACLE AVOIDANCE GRID

RECHARGE STATUS

GNK
POWER DROID

Power droids are walking batteries designed to recharge other droids, vehicles, and machines. A power droid walking around Mos Eisley sees the world in terms of power levels and energy sources.

R2-D2

R2-D2 is programmed to navigate starships through outer space, even during ferocious space battles. To do this, his visual sensors must have many functions. He can be linked up to computer databases detailing star charts and vehicle data.

A PILOT'S BEST FRIEND

R2-D2's holographic camera is designed to display 3-D representations of space battles so the pilot can identify enemies and plot his course. The technology can also be used to record secret messages.

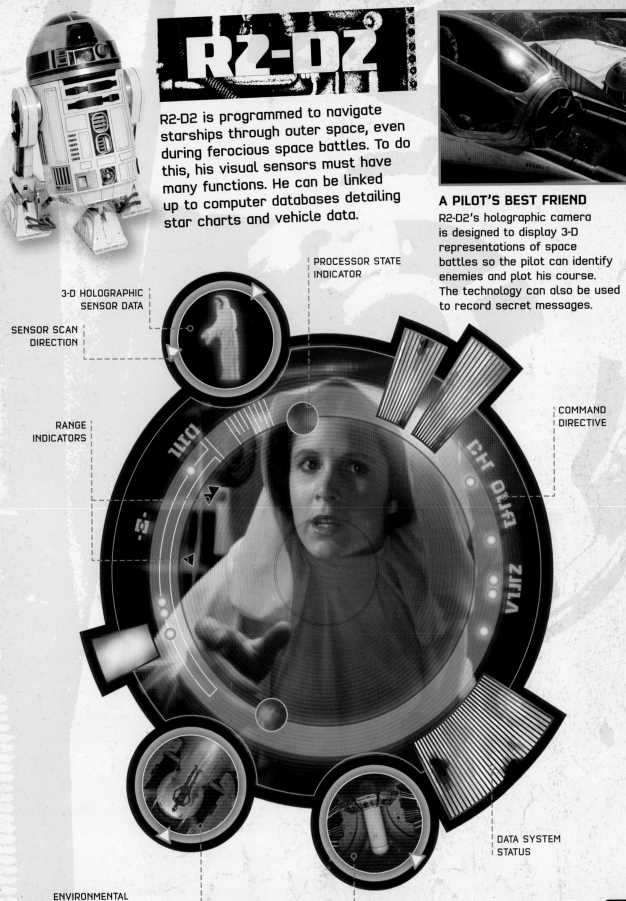

PROCESSOR STATE INDICATOR

3-D HOLOGRAPHIC SENSOR DATA

SENSOR SCAN DIRECTION

RANGE INDICATORS

COMMAND DIRECTIVE

DATA SYSTEM STATUS

ENVIRONMENTAL SENSOR

IG-88

Rogue assassin droid IG-88 has eyes in the back of his head. Rear and front optical sensors allow him to see in every direction at once, so he can be aware of any danger. When he is hired by Darth Vader to capture Han Solo, IG-88 also makes use of other sensors, which allow him to sense movement, register temperature, and see through metal. He uses his multi-faceted vision and his databanks to identify rival bounty hunters and potential targets.

DIRECTIVE PARAMETERS

WEAPON DETECTION

VOICE STRESS ANALYSIS

BATTLE DROID

Battle droids' visual sensors are no sharper than the eyes of an average living being, but the droids' programming allows them to distinguish between friends and foes, and seek out targets and objectives, as identified by their Droid Control Ship. Such abilities are useful during a furious and fast-paced battle, when droids need to make split-second decisions.

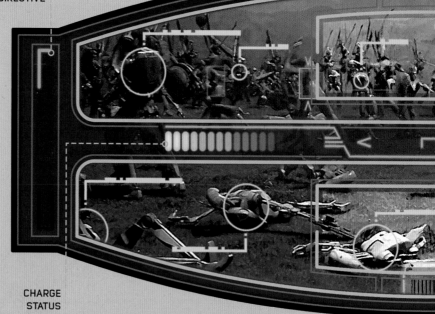

PRIMARY MODE DIRECTIVE

CHARGE STATUS

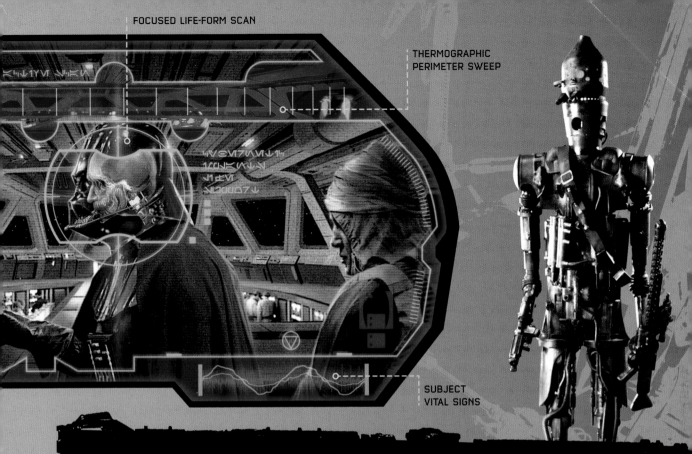

FOCUSED LIFE-FORM SCAN

THERMOGRAPHIC
PERIMETER SWEEP

SUBJECT
VITAL SIGNS

DROID VISION: COMBAT

OPPOSITION
IDENTIFIER

COMMAND
SIGNAL

Combat droids are
fitted with multiple
visual sensors and
data displays.
They need to keep
track of many things
at once, including
targets and threats.

UNIT ID

E-5 BLASTER

NOT SCARED OF BIGGER DROIDS

R2-D2 isn't programmed for combat, but you should never dismiss him as just a "stupid little astro-droid." Two super battle droids make this mistake on board General Grievous's ship, the *Invisible Hand*. Before the super battle droids realize what's happening, R2 sets them on fire and flies to safety.

WHY SHOULD YOU NEVER UNDERESTIMATE R2-D2?

DISTRACTING DROID

Obi-Wan Kenobi and Anakin Skywalker are captured on Grievous's ship. Suddenly, R2-D2 activates many of his systems, creating a noisy spectacle. While the battle droids are distracted, Obi-Wan and Anakin swing into action and grab their lightsabers!

SMOKESCREEN

R2 and his friends are being chased by stormtroopers on Cloud City! R2-D2 activates his fire extinguisher, filling the air with a cloud of super-cold vapor. The stormtroopers can't see through the murky fire-suppression gas, giving the Rebels time to reach the safety of Han Solo's starship, the *Millennium Falcon*.

R2-D2'S BARREL-SHAPED body contains many tools for repairing starships and helping pilots and mechanics—but the feisty little astromech is rather creative in finding other uses for his tools. When he finds himself in danger, R2 can always come up with a way to defeat or distract the enemies who are threatening him or his friends.

DROID ATTACK!

BATTLE DROIDS
VS
LIGHTSABER

A Jedi like Obi-Wan Kenobi can use his lightsaber to slice right through battle droids' flimsy bodies or to deflect their blaster fire right back at them!

PROBE DROID
VS
BLASTER

Probe droids are big, sneaky, and scary, but with a well-aimed blaster shot, Han Solo causes the probot enough concern that it self-destructs!

CRAB DROID
VS
BLASTER RIFLE

Separatist crab droids are fast, tough, and deadly, but the Republic's clone troopers know how to locate a droid's weak points—like the top of its head!

The bigger the droid, the harder it is to destroy. Jedi Knights aren't worried about battle droids, but giant Separatist droids require much greater firepower.

HAILFIRE DROID
VS
REPUBLIC ATTACK GUNSHIP

HOMING SPIDER DROID
VS
AT-TE

Hailfire droids are deadly mobile tanks that demolish enemy troops with their powerful missiles. These speedy Separatist units are best defeated from the air, so the Republic army attacks with laser cannons from their gunships.

Homing spider droids can blast rows of clone troopers or raise their guns to fire at gunships overhead. The Republic strikes back with squads of tough, heavily armed AT-TEs, which take aim at a spider droid's legs or laser dish to destroy it.

HOW DOES C-3PO RELAX?

DROIDS DON'T GET tired like living beings do—but they still need to recharge and repair. C-3PO is programmed to interact with humans, so he sometimes behaves as if he is a tired life-form who needs to take a break from the worry and stress of his daily existence.

PLAYING IT SAFE
Some droids relax by playing and watching games, but C-3PO is more interested in safety as he watches Chewbacca and R2-D2 play a game of Dejarik aboard the *Millennium Falcon*. When Chewbacca becomes angry at R2-D2, Han Solo warns C-3PO that Wookiees sometimes tear their opponents' arms off when they lose. Now all C-3PO can think about is making sure R2 lets the Wookiee win!

QUIET TIME

After C-3PO loses an arm in a fall on Tatooine, Luke Skywalker repairs the golden droid. C-3PO shuts down for a little while so his damaged systems will repair more quickly.

A LONG SOAK

After Owen Lars buys him from Jawa traders, C-3PO isn't very happy to be stuck on a moisture farm. But at least he has time to take a soothing oil bath. His joints are full of Tatooine's sand and grit!

KIND MASTER

Luke Skywalker lowers his uncle's new protocol droid, C-3PO, into an oil bath. He knows that a happy droid is a helpful droid.

Medical DROIDS

VISUAL SENSORS

COMPUTER INTERFACE

VARIOUS TOOLS PLUG INTO ARM

2-1B

BLOOD TRANSFUSION CANISTER

DEAR DOCTOR

2-1B droids perform tasks ranging from routine check-ups to emergency surgery, helping civilians as well as soldiers. They are programmed to speak calmly, which reassures patients.

INJECTOR ARM

FX-6

HANDY ASSISTANT

FX droids help both robot and living doctors figure out what's wrong with patients and assist with surgery. They don't talk, but display words on their video screens.

CARING

On Polis Massa, a gentle midwife droid helps Padmé Amidala through the birth of her and Anakin's twins, Luke and Leia. The midwife droid ensures that the babies are healthy and safe, even though she cannot save Padmé.

ECHO BASE DOCTOR

After Luke Skywalker nearly dies in a blizzard on Hoth, a 2-1B droid supervises his treatment. He places Luke in a healing bacta tank until he is sure that the Jedi is fully recovered.

MIDWIFE DROID

Medical droids are robot doctors, whose memory banks are crammed full of information about diseases and injuries. They know how to treat thousands of different species. Galactic citizens rely on medical droids for both routine and emergency care.

MEDICAL DROID

MANUFACTURER: VARIOUS
HEIGHT: VARIES
GENDER: VARIES
FEATURES: MEDICAL TOOLS, INTEGRATED DISEASE DATABASE, NUTRIENT FLUIDS, PROGRAMMED FOR PRECISION, SOOTHING VOICE (MIDWIFE DROIDS)

DROIDS GONE WRONG

Droids are supposed to obey their programming, but software errors or bad wiring can cause malfunctions that turn droids into liars, thieves, or worse. Unscrupulous owners have also been known to reprogram their droids to do harm to others. Such renegade droids are rare, but living beings greatly fear them.

GAS CANISTERS

IG-88

MODIFIED E-11 BLASTER

DAMAGE-RESISTANT SERVO WIRING

ROGUE ROBOT

The IG-series of assassin droids was produced by Holowan Mechanicals, which also created MagnaGuards. When activated, the first IG-88 unit destroyed its creators because it viewed them as a threat. IG-88 became a rogue droid, operating under his own orders in search of profit.

IG-88 is one of an elite group of bounty hunters hired by Darth Vader to locate and capture the *Millennium Falcon*.

INSECTILE HEAD

DANGEROUS DROID

4-LOM is a protocol droid who originally worked as a valet on a luxury spaceliner. The crafty droid overwrote his own programming and became a jewel thief. As a rogue droid, 4-LOM was free to pursue his own evil agenda, eventually becoming a deadly bounty hunter.

RUSTY DROID PLATING

4-LOM

8D8

CAPTIVE POWER DROID

METAL MONSTER

8D8 droids work in metal-smelting plants where it's too hot for living beings. An 8D8 droid was purchased by Jabba the Hutt and reprogrammed to torment other droids in Jabba's palace. He works together with EV-9D9.

LEVER FOR PORTABLE SMELTER

SADISTIC SUPERVISOR

MerenData accidentally built its EV supervisor droids with parts from interrogation droids. This made the EV-series malfunction and act cruelly to those under their supervision. EV-9D9 escaped capture and was soon employed by Jabba the Hutt to oversee the droids in his palace. Beware!

EV-9D9

DROID COMMAND CONSOLE

SPINDLY LIMBS

ARE DROIDS ALWAYS RESPECTED?

SOME PEOPLE ARE kind to droids, but many are not. These people do what they like with droids without caring about them. The galaxy is a scary place for droids. Everywhere you look, someone is ready to sell you, trade you, or—worst of all—melt you down!

DON'T SPILL!
R2-D2 is a sophisticated droid built to repair starships and talk to computers, but Jabba the Hutt makes him wear a tray and serve drinks. R2, however, doesn't mind: he knows that this is all part of a plan to rescue Han Solo. The little droid has Luke Skywalker's lightsaber concealed inside his dome!

DIRTY WORK

C-3PO speaks millions of languages and can help diplomats during important meetings. But after Luke gives him to Jabba as a gift, C-3PO is forced to translate rude threats made by bounty hunters. And when Jabba doesn't like what he hears, he takes his anger out on his "talk droid." C-3PO often finds himself covered in green slime from Jabba's dinner!

GATHERING DUST

Captured by Jawas, C-3PO and R2-D2 find themselves surrounded by battered, broken droids inside a sandcrawler. The Jawas plan to sell these droids, but in the meantime, they are piled up and left to rust—as if they were scrap metal. C-3PO and R2 hope they don't end up like that!

After Count Dooku cut off Anakin's arm, Anakin replaced the lost limb with a mechanical one, hidden by a black glove.

DROID
Anakin's right hand and part of his forearm are mechanical.
TOTAL: 10%

NOT DROID
The rest of Anakin is flesh and blood— at least until his duel with Obi-Wan Kenobi.
TOTAL: 90%

WAT TAMBOR

A member of the Separatist Council, Wat Tambor wears an environment suit that mimics the high pressure of his home planet, Skako.

DROID
Tambor looks like a droid, but he is actually a living being in protective gear.
TOTAL: 0%

NOT DROID
Skakoans like Wat are used to higher pressure and an atmosphere rich in methane.
TOTAL: 100%

DROID OR NOT?

LOBOT

Lobot is chief aide to Cloud City's Baron Lando Calrissian. His brain is connected directly to his city's central computer.

DROID
Lobot's implant attaches to his brain, allowing him to talk to Cloud City's computers just by thinking.
TOTAL: 10%

NOT DROID
Lobot is a living being, but he prefers to communicate using his thoughts instead of actually speaking.
TOTAL: 90%

After nearly being killed in a duel with Obi-Wan Kenobi, Vader is fitted with artificial limbs and life-supporting armor. He cannot survive without them.

DROID
Vader's arms and legs are mechanical, as are some of his organs. Machines help him breathe, see, hear, and speak.

TOTAL: 80%

NOT DROID
Vader may have forgotten the feel of rain or fresh air, but beneath his armor some of his humanity still remains.

TOTAL: 20%

DARTH VADER

DROID
Grievous's limbs, body, and even parts of his head are artificial.

TOTAL: 95%

Grievous was once a Kaleesh warlord, but since being injured in an explosion, most of his body has been replaced by armored parts.

NOT DROID
Grievous's eyes, brain, spinal cord, and organs are organic. Be warned, he hates being called a droid!

TOTAL: 5%

Some beings look like droids, but they are really cyborgs; living beings with mechanical parts. Sometimes, these parts replace lost limbs or organs, and sometimes they make a life-form stronger or faster. But remember: just because a cyborg is part-robot, it doesn't make him a droid!

GENERAL GRIEVOUS

B'OMARR MONK

The B'omarr monks live in Jabba the Hutt's palace. They have thrown away their bodies so their brains can live forever in jars.

DROID
The monks' brain-jars are carried in modified droids that look like huge spiders.

TOTAL: 99%

NOT DROID
The brain floating in its nutrient fluid is all that remains of the monk's body.

TOTAL: 1%

MAGNAGUARD

MANUFACTURER: HOLOWAN MECHANICALS

HEIGHT: 1.95 M (6 FT 5 IN)

GENDER: MALE PROGRAMMING

FEATURES: SENSORS, COMBAT PROGRAMMING

LOSING HIS HEAD

When a MagnaGuard attacks Obi-Wan Kenobi, the Jedi cuts off the droid's head. However, MagnaGuards have an extra electronic eye in their chests, enabling them to keep fighting —even without their heads!

IG-102

BATTLE SCARS

Previous battles with the Jedi have left their mark on Grievous's guards: their cloaks are torn, while their metal faces and bodies bear lightsaber scars. Scary!

SECONDARY PHOTORECEPTOR

DON'T TOUCH!
The glowing tips of MagnaGuards' electrostaffs can stun or kill. Electrostaffs are made of phrik, a tough metal that resists even a lightsaber's cutting power.

DEADLY ELECTROSTAFF

DURASTEEL LIMBS

DARK DEFENDERS
MagnaGuards protect General Grievous on the planet Utapau. Obi-Wan Kenobi must defeat these grim bodyguards before he can duel Grievous himself.

IG-101

MAGNETIC FEET

MAGNAGUARDS

Terrifying MagnaGuards protect the Separatists' most important leaders, such as Count Dooku and General Grievous. Their advanced combat programming makes them very dangerous indeed. MagnaGuards are specially programmed to attack and destroy Jedi Knights

SERVING THE DARK SIDE

Droids' actions are determined by their programming—they have no choice. Some droids become servants of the dark side because they are designed for evil purposes, or because their masters order them to.

"CHOPPER" DROID

These medical droids got their grim nickname by operating on living beings to give them artificial limbs and organs. Choppers help entomb Darth Vader in his life-preserving armor.

VIPER PROBE DROID

Probe droids have been used by military forces for centuries. The Empire dispatches frightening, black-armored probots to hunt for Luke Skywalker and his Rebel friends.

ASN-121 ASSASSIN DROID

The bounty hunter Zam Wesell sends this flying assassin droid to Padmé Amidala's apartment, where it releases poisonous kouhun insects into her bedroom.

SITH PROBE DROID

Darth Maul sends three "dark eye" probes across Tatooine in search of Padmé Amidala and her Jedi companions. These small droids can search for their targets while hovering above crowds.

IT-0 INTERROGATION DROID

These cruel droids are programmed to terrify the Empire's prisoners. They have mechanical arms tipped with frightening tools, which often intimidate the prisoners into revealing their deepest secrets.

RA-7 PROTOCOL DROID

These grim-faced protocol droids are so common aboard the Death Star that they are nicknamed "Death Star droids." They secretly spy on their masters to make sure they stay loyal to the Empire.

IMPERIAL ASTROMECHS

Astromech droids serve the pilots and mechanics of the Empire, too. R2-Q5 and R5-J2 are two of the droids waiting aboard the second Death Star to greet Emperor Palpatine when he visits the station during construction above the green Endor Moon.

DO DROIDS HAVE FRIENDS?

MOST CITIZENS OF THE galaxy rarely wonder what their droids are thinking or feeling. And most droids only do what they're programmed to do; they don't talk to others unless they need to. But sometimes droids do form friendships, either with other droids, or with living beings who don't just treat them like machines.

DROID DATA

■ Most droids receive regular memory wipes, so they often don't remember things they've said or done. Droids are more likely to develop personalities if their masters don't erase their memories.

GETTING ALONG
Chewbacca often gets annoyed because C-3PO complains about everything, while C-3PO thinks Chewie should control his temper better. But Chewie tries to repair C-3PO after stormtroopers blast him on Cloud City. C-3PO gets angry when he realizes his head is on backward, but deep down is grateful for the Wookiee's efforts.

EWOK FRIEND

Feisty little R2-D2 is annoyed when the Ewoks take him and his friends prisoner, and he tries to zap the furry creatures with electric shocks. But after he calms down, R2 finds that he's quite fond of Wicket. The Ewok is small but brave—just like R2.

PARTNERS IN BATTLE

Most starship pilots view their astro-droids as pieces of equipment. But Anakin Skywalker has known R2-D2 for many years, and thinks of him as a trusty friend. Anakin can often understand the little droid's whistles and beeps, which helps them work as team, both in space and on land.

SAVING THE GALAXY

Most droids spend their days doing the dull jobs they are assigned by their owners. But some droids have a higher calling: R2-D2 and C-3PO help their masters save the galaxy from evil!

A CALL FOR HELP
When General Grievous kidnaps Chancellor Palpatine, Anakin Skywalker and Obi-Wan Kenobi race to save the Republic's leader. They are trapped inside an elevator on Grievous's starship, and call R2-D2 for help. Can he get the elevator running again?

CAUGHT IN A TRAP
Luke Skywalker and Han Solo disguise themselves as stormtroopers on their mission to rescue Princess Leia from the Death Star. However, all three of them—and Chewie—end up trapped in a trash masher. Can R2 stop the compactor before the Rebel heroes are crushed?

AVOIDING THE GUARDS
On the moon of Endor, Han, Leia, and Chewbacca lead a mission to destroy the energy shield that protects the second Death Star. They must break into an Imperial bunker, but it is heavily guarded by stormtroopers.

DROID TO THE RESCUE!

R2-D2 knows Obi-Wan and Anakin need him, but he's got bigger problems: two hulking super battle droids are searching for him. R2 defeats the droids easily and then races off to rescue the Jedi. He receives Obi-Wan's instructions via his comlink and takes control of the elevator with his computer interface arm.

QUICK THINKING

While C-3PO urges his friend to hurry, R2-D2 taps into the Death Star's computer network, locates the garbage compactors, and shuts them down. The Rebels are saved with just moments to spare! C-3PO should be relieved when he hears his friends yelling happily, but the anxious droid thinks they are screaming in pain!

INTO THE WOODS

C-3PO and R2-D2 distract as many stormtroopers as they can and lead them on a chase through the woods. Endor's Ewok warriors are ready to ambush the troopers, giving Han and Leia a chance to destroy the energy shield before the Rebel fleet arrives to attack the Death Star.

GLOSSARY

BACTA

- A healing chemical substance used in hospitals across the galaxy.

BATTLE OF CORUSCANT

- Clone Wars conflict in 19 BBY, in which the Separatist army attacks the planet Coruscant and kidnaps Supreme Chancellor Palpatine.

BATTLE OF ENDOR

- Conflict in 4 ABY, in which the Rebel Alliance attacks Imperial forces on the moon of Endor, resulting in the destruction of the second Death Star and decline of the Empire.

BATTLE OF GEONOSIS

- Conflict in 22 BBY, in which the Republic's Clone Army attacks the Separatists' Droid Army on the planet Geonosis, marking the start of the Clone Wars.

BATTLE OF KASHYYYK

- Conflict in 19 BBY, in which the Separatists' Droid Army fights against the Wookiees and Jedi on the planet Kashyyyk.

BATTLE OF NABOO

- Conflict in 32 BBY, in which the Trade Federation invades the planet Naboo with their Droid Army.

BATTLE OF YAVIN

- Conflict in Year 0, in which Rebel forces, based on the moon Yavin 4, attack and destroy the first Imperial Death Star.

BLOCKADE

- Something that blocks access to something else. For example, a political strategy that prevents food and resources from reaching a specific destination.

BOUNTY HUNTER

- Someone who tracks down, captures, or destroys wanted people for a fee.

CLONE ARMY

- An army of genetically identical soldiers, all trained to be perfect warriors. They fight for the Republic.

CLONE WARS

- A series of galaxy-wide battles fought between the Republic's Clone Army and the Separatists' Droid Army, which takes place from 22–19 BBY.

COLICOID

- An insectoid species from the planet Colla IV who are hired to create several battlefield droids for the Separatists.

CORUSCANT

- The capital of the Republic. This planet is home to the Senate building, the Jedi Temple, and the Jedi Council.

CYBORG

- A being that is partly a living organism and partly a droid.

DEATH STAR

- A planet-sized Imperial battle station, which has enough firepower to destroy an entire planet.

DIPLOMAT

- A person who conducts negotiations and builds relationships with people from other planets or cultures.

DRONE

- A worker who obeys the orders of others and has no authority of his own.

ECHO BASE

- The headquarters of the Rebel Alliance, located on the ice planet Hoth.

ELECTROSTAFF

- Weapon favored by General Grievous and his MagnaGuard bodyguards.

EMPEROR

■ Ruler of the Empire.

EMPIRE

■ A cruel power that rules the galaxy from 19 BBY–4 ABY under the leadership of Emperor Palpatine, a Sith Lord.

FORCE

■ The energy that flows through all living things. It can be used for good, by studying the light side—or for evil, by studying the dark side.

GEONOSIS

■ A rocky, desert planet in the Outer Rim Territories, famous for its droid factories.

GUNGANS

■ An amphibious species from the planet Naboo.

GYROSCOPE

■ A spinning device that helps objects maintain their balance.

HOTH

■ An ice-covered planet located in a remote sector of the Outer Rim Territories.

HYPERSPACE

■ An extra dimension of space, used by experienced starship pilots to travel faster than the speed of light using a hyperdrive.

JAWAS

■ A species of small creatures native to the planet Tatooine. They trade scrap metal found in the desert.

JEDI

■ A member of the Jedi Order who studies the light side of the Force in pursuit of peace and justice.

JEDI PURGE

■ The attempt by Chancellor Palpatine in 19 BBY to destroy the entire Jedi Order.

LIGHTSABER

■ A weapon with a blade of pure energy that is used by Jedi and Sith warriors.

NABOO

■ A beautiful planet near the border of the Outer Rim Territories.

PODRACING

■ A popular sport in which competitors race against each other in high-powered vehicles called Podracers.

PROBE DROID

■ An Imperial robot that gathers and transmits data.

REBEL ALLIANCE

■ The organization that resists and fights against the Empire.

REPUBLIC

■ The elected government of the galaxy, under leadership of the Chancellor.

SANDCRAWLER

■ A large transport vehicle that travels well over sand, often used by Jawa tribes as mobile bases.

SENATE

■ Government of the Republic, with representatives from all parts of the galaxy.

SENATOR

■ A person who represents their planet, sector, or system in the Senate.

SEPARATISTS

■ An alliance against the Republic. Also known as the Confederacy of Independent Systems.

SITH

■ An ancient sect of Force-sensitives who study the dark side to gain control and succeed in their greedy plans.

TATOOINE

■ A desert planet with two suns located in the Outer Rim Territories. Known as a meeting place for criminals and smugglers.

TRADE FEDERATION

■ A bureaucratic organization that controls much of the trade and commerce in the galaxy.

INDEX

Characters are listed under their most frequently used common name, for example Luke Skywalker is found under "L" and "Darth Vader" is under "D."

Main entries are in bold.

LONDON, NEW YORK, MELBOURNE,
MUNICH, AND DELHI

For Dorling Kindersley
Editor Shari Last
Additional Editors Julia March, Helen Murray
Designers Clive Savage, Lisa Sodeau,
Rhys Thomas, Toby Truphet
Design Manager Ron Stobbart
Publishing Manager Catherine Saunders
Art Director Lisa Lanzarini
Publisher Simon Beecroft
Publishing Director Alex Allan
Production Editor Siu Yin Chan
Production Controller Kara Wallace

For Lucasfilm
Executive Editor J. W. Rinzler
Art Director Troy Alders
Keeper of the Holocron Leland Chee
Director of Publishing Carol Roeder

First published in the United States in 2012
by DK Publishing
375 Hudson Street, New York, New York 10014

10 9 8 7 6 5 4 3 2 1
001–182946–Apr/12

A catalog record for this book is available
from the Library of Congress.

ISBN: 978-0-7566-9015-1

Color reproduction by Media Development Printing Ltd, UK
Printed and bound by Hung Hing, China

The publisher would like to thank Chris Reiff and Chris
Trevas for their artwork on pages 66–69 and Jo Casey
for her editorial assistance. Lucasfilm would like to
thank Jann Moorhead and David Anderman.

Discover more at
www.dk.com
www.starwars.com